SAVAGE REALMS MONTHLY

FEBRUARY: VOLUME 1

B. HARLAN CRAWFORD   WILLARD BLACK

ALEXANDER S KARCHER

LITERARY REBEL, LLC

FOREWORD

FROM THE EDITOR'S DESK

Welcome, dear reader, to the February issue of Savage Realms Monthly (a little late).

This month's issue is focused on, you guessed it, savage warriors, life or death conflict, and ages undreamed of. We've got three great stories for you , along with author interviews and more original artwork. One story is a continuation of Redgar and Natali's adventures from January, the other two are wholly unique tales never before published outside Savage Realms.

Our mission here at Savage Realms Monthly is not only to highlight the best in sword and sorcery fiction, but also to give a platform to new and developing authors. We searched high and low for the following adventure tales and we think you'll like what we are bringing to print this month.

So sharpen your battle axe and dig in!

IN THE COVE OF THE APOSTATES

BY B. HARLAN CRAWFORD

A SINEWY MAN in a crude loincloth picked his way along a boulder-strewn beach. His age was hard to tell. His hair was white but his pale, beardless face was not yet creased with age. He squinted against the sunlight as he took in the azure waters of the secluded cove which lay west of Mcorro-Tanj. He kept casting nervous glances at a tottering villa perched atop a rocky cliff.

In one weathered hand he gripped his bronze-headed mace as he approached a crude awning was pitched just above the high tide mark. There was no sign of an occupant and after a half-hearted halloo he rummaged through the meager belongings, uncovering a thread bare tunic of Indigo linen, a pair of battered sandals, and a wickedly curved saber in a shagreen girdle. Then his eyes fell on a bloated wineskin hanging from the makeshift tent pole.

He regarded this last item for a heartbeat before seizing it and taking a long draught. The wine was of the highest quality and he drank with relish.

"Make free with my wine!"

He turned, wine running down his chin, in time to see woman emerge from the waves. She was tall and robust with thick sinews coiling beneath sun-bronzed skin. Black hair hung in wet tangles around bare shoulders and she gripped a net bulging with a coral-encrusted lump.

"Blood of Nuada!" he exclaimed.

"That's not an oath I've heard before." Her tone was conversational, but there was a wolfish menace to her movements and she had the eyes of a killer.

The man shuddered at her approach. She was like a she-demon vomited up from the depths of hell.

"Is Nuada the god of your people?"

"My people are long gone." he stammered. "I am the last. We were once lords of this land. I am Hafgan, I dwell in the caves, yonder."

He gestured toward the rocky crags rising in the distance.

The woman was withing striking distance now and dripping with seawater.

"I am Seanai," she told him, "of Ibak."

Hafgan was vaguely aware of the land called Ibak, a frigid waste inhabited by star-headed sorcerers and cannibalistic troglodytes.

"I spied the tent pitched on the beach," he said. "I came to issue a warning."

Seanai glanced meaningfully at the wineskin in his hand. "Your warning must be grim indeed if you must fortify yourself with wine."

"My life is an austere and wine is difficult to come by."

"I will not begrudge you then."

Seanai dropped her net and set about pulling the tunic over her wet flesh. Hafgan pulled his eyes away and noticed for the first time the object swathed in the net. It was a sculpted head, broken away from a larger statue. The carved face was androgynously beautiful, yet the artist had carved some strange eccentricity in the almond-shaped eyes and the full lips lent the countenance a subtle, disturbing grotesqueness. The wildly colorful coral encrusting the head accentuated its peculiarity. Hafgan cried out in horror and Seanai, still struggling to arrange her tunic, jerked about with a start.

"Loins of Jhullah-Jhulku! What ails you, man?"

Hafgan gesticulated at the head.

"How did you get that?"

Seanai nodded toward the waves. "I was diving for crabs and in the depths I found ruins; towers, domes, and columned temples, all heavily overgrown with coral. Even at that depth, the colors were bright and vibrant! There were hues I have never seen before, nor have I names for them." She paused and gazed at the water. "I would have dived deeper and explored that wondrous city, but my lungs were ready to burst."

Hafgan's face contorted. "It is about that city I came to warn you. To violate that dread site will surely bring doom."

"How so?"

Hafgan made a sign to ward off evil. "My race built that city eons ago. Mighty were my ancestors! Mighty, clever and beautiful! They made obeisance to Nuada, god of sea and storm, and he blessed them. My people prospered and folk from all corners of the earth came to pay tribute and behold the wonders of the city.

"But some said Nuada was miserly with his blessings, and that the people should instead exalt Aadank, a fiend from the outer dark! Derided at first, these heretics persevered, and their blasphemy spread among the people like a plague. In time, all revered Aadank.

"Aadank demanded grim tribute and to gather such tribute my ancestors made war upon their neighbors, committing foul abominations. At last, Nuada's anger fell upon them. He plunged the city into the depths and bestowed a curse on its people! Though they drowned, they would never taste death! Eternally they lie among the ruins, contemplating their folly."

Hafgan trembled, breathing heavily, as though telling this tale tasked him. He took another long pull from the wineskin.

By now Seanai had dressed and armed herself. Adjusting the saber in her belt, she scowled at the hermit. "My taking the head angers Nuada?"

"Nay, it angers the spirits of the Apostates, those cursed by Nuada to eternally haunt the sunken city. And you must beware! They have learned to reach beyond their tomb to punish transgressors."

Seanai shrugged, picked up the head and carried it to the surf. With some effort she hurled it into the cove. It soared a good distance before plunging into the water.

"That's that," she stated.

Hafgan was not satisfied. "You compound your sin with mockery! They will come for you now! Just as they-"

Seanai shushed him. "I thirst, and since you have laid claim to my wine, I must get more. I have a cache laid in at yon ruin, come!"

Hafgan followed the Ibakeen along the beach, then up a rocky path to the old house.

"You have been inside the manse then? I thought I saw light flickering within last night."

"I have dwelt there for two- nay, four nights."

"Do you think to make the place your home?"

"For a time," she said. "I need respite from civilized life."

Seanai pulled open the creaking front door and stepped inside. Hafgan followed, grateful for the shade. He was more accustomed to a cave than the blazing sun and his shoulders were beginning to turn red.

Beyond the door lay a parlor, once resplendent, now falling to ruin. Most of its finery had long since rotted away. A battered mosaic covering the floor, depicting frolicking sea-nymphs, and an ornate fireplace spoke to the room's former splendor. The staircase ascending was reduced to a pile of rotten lumber and replaced by a knotted rope. Scattered crates and barrels served as furniture, along with a crude wooden workbench littered with mauls, mallets, chisels and other woodworking tools.

Dominating the center of the old parlor was a peculiar cask-like object formed of wood and treated leather. It was the size of a rowboat, but it's top was completely covered, with no opening anywhere along its surface. Seanai grasped an iron ring on top and opened a trapdoor. Reaching inside, she extracted another wineskin. She drank, wiped her lips with the back of one hand, turned and grinned. "I know not what this thing is meant to be, but it makes a fine wine cellar!"

"The last inhabitant of this house built it. He was a magus from the east. He meant to plunder the sunken city with it. I warned him against it, as is my mandate, but he would have none of it. He disappeared before he had a chance to try his artifice, taken by the Apostates no doubt."

"When was this?"

"Some ten winters ago."

Seanai pondered that for a moment, regarding the

strange boat with furrowed brow. Finally, she shook her raven hair and snorted. "Bah! He must have been addled, or a lotus-eater."

"Why do you not flee, woman? Do you not fear death at the hands of the Apostates?"

The Ibakeen shrugged. "I should have died many times. Yet I live."

"Who are your people? What race spawns women of such stature that go armed as men?"

"The people of Ibak dwell in the shadow of constant death, menaced on all sides by horrors. We do not have the luxury of coddling our women the way civilized men do."

Seanai went to the fireplace and replaced the smoldering embers with pieces of driftwood and detritus from the mansion. She soon had a cheery blaze in the hearth. "But life in Ibak is gloomy," she said. "Therefore I fled. I have roamed far and wide since."

"How come you to the cove?"

"I sailed with a pirate galley out of Kairoon. things went well enough for a space, unbuttil the captain and his mate were too handsy. I leapt overboard when we rounded the Horn of Tazzozz."

Hafgan started. "Tazzozz lays many leagues from here!"

"I was pulled from the sea by Tanjeet fishermen who bore me to their village. The Tanjeet are excellent wine-makers but too prudish for my tastes, so I availed myself of several skins and wandered down the beach until I came upon this ruin."

"These waters hold aught but doom."

"We shall see." Seanai threw herself down upon a pile of threadbare linens close to the fire. "For now I intend to relax and enjoy this wine. You may stay and share my fire and wine, but mind your manners and trouble me no more with talk of Apostates."

Hafgan grumbled and sat down opposite the Ibakeen, who laughed heartily.

"Good! Now hearken and I will regale you with a tale of the deadly pygmies of DraPaugh!"

As Seanai began her tale, the sun set, and dark clouds gathered over the cove.

It was close to midnight when a brilliant flash of lightning, followed by a stentorian thunderclap, roused Senai from slumber. She was wide and awake and alert instantly, as is the habit of the savage. Some instinct drew her to the shuttered window. Catlike, she rose and crept toward it and peered outside. Seanai precieved a shape, darker than the surrounding gloom, lurking outside the window. Before she could react, another lightning bolt crawled across the heavens, illuminating the figure for a heartbeat.

It was a shambling mass of coral, barnacles, and other sea-life. From the lump atop its shoulders peered the smooth, impassive, alabaster face of a handsome young man. The torso and limbs were made from fragments of mismatched statuary. One arm was that of a warrior with an armored bracer, the other resembled the smooth flesh of a woman. One leg was that of an athletic youth, while the other belonged to a majestic war-horse. Articulating this hodgepodge of stone limbs was a writhing mass of sea-life. A massive starfish made up the left knee, a grotesquely stretched octopus manipulated the right shoulder. Swarms of shrimps and jellies worked the neck and wrists. More octopi and cuttlefish served as hands, each gripping shards of coral and stone.

Seanai recoiled with a curse, snatching up her saber and waking Hafgan with her foot. "Rise, hermit, and gird your loins! there is deviltry afoot!"

He sat upright, mace in hand and croaked, "The Apostates?"

"So it would seem. Some horrid pile of sea-offal lurks at the window. Help me with the door!"

They barred the entry with a heavy timber and barricaded it with barrels and crates for good measure. Having re-kindled a decent blaze on the hearth, Seanai went once more to the window. The Apostate still lingered outside while shadowy forms could be seen in tow. Beyond were more flashes of lightning in the roiling black clouds.

"Hafgan, you say these things attacked this house before?"

"Ten years ago, when they took the magus. I know not how. I stayed in my cave and did not bear witness."

"You'll bear witness now by Jhullah-Jhulku! Pray to your gods this old shack can-"

The gods chose to mock the Ibakeen at that moment, for the Apostate smashed the shuttered window with a stupendous blow. Cursing, Seanai slashed at its head only for her blade to turn against the sculpted marble. The thing struck again, knocking Seanai to her knees. The Apostate then seized her by the hair and tried to drag her through the window.

Hafgan leapt forward and brought his mace down on the patchwork horror, shattering its arms and scattering sea creatures. Suddenly freed, Seanai seized a maul from the workbench, smashed it into her enemy's chest and it fell backwards through the window.

With a thunderous report the front door shivered as apostates hurled themselves against it. The door sagged, the planks splintered and the wood burst inward. Two Apostates stumbled into the room and fell, three others strode into the parlor. Seanai and Hafgan rained mighty blows on their attackers, knocking great chunks of stone from heads, chest, and arms, but the monsters pressed forward.

"The legs," shouted Hafgan. "Break their legs!"

They turned their attention to the legs, trying to cripple the sea-spawned horrors while avoiding crushing fists. Soon Seanai was bleeding from myriad cuts and Hafgan slumped, his breath coming in ragged gasps and his attacks slowing.

Seanai and the hermit fell back, deeper into the chamber, in an effort to catch their breath, but more Apostates smashed through the front wall of the house. These were more repulsively elaborate than the previous lot, wildly festooned with colorful coral and sponges and a cold, brine-laden wind followed them.

"We cannot win!" shouted Seanai. "Up that rope to the floor above, we'll see how the bastards climb!"

Hafgan obeyed, shimmying up the rope. Seanai came up next, using her legs and one arm, unwilling to relinquish her hold on the maul. Clambering onto the floor above, she hastily drew up the rope and the Apostates milled about below, unsure of how to reach their prey.

The second floor was in even worse repair. Once it had several rooms, but the walls had collapsed, leaving one great chamber with a square hole in the floor. Two great windows looked out on the angry sea. A waxed cloth had been tacked over them, but it was in tatters, twisting with the wind.

Hafgan, his eyes ablaze with a fanatical glare and heedless of the gale, strode to the windows and stared out upon the raging ocean. A mighty gust blew through the windows with such force that it rattled the timbers of the old villa and pelted the walls with stinging salt spray. Hafgan took a step back, giving way before the gust, then pressed forward, closer to the window, his jaw set in defiance.

"There are eight of them below!" Seanai cried. She was crouched above the hole in the floor and the illumination from the fire gave her a hellish countenance. She came to stand at Hafgan's side. "At worst, we run the rope out one of these windows and make a break for it. I dislike the idea of retreat, but they are sluggish and clumsy. We should be able to- Damnation!"

Another gust pelted her with salt spray. "It's a moot point if this gale brings the old shack down on our heads!"

Hafgan threw his arms wide and howled. "Nuada! Hear me! The Apostates offended you and they are punished eternally! We, their offspring, have done penance for their sins! Is this not enough? Why punish this woman? The sins of the Apostates are not hers! Thou art an unjust god! I, Hafgan, the last of your sentinels, rebuke thee! Hear me Nuada! I rebuke thee!"

A great thunderclap sounded and arcs of lightning rippled across the sky.

Hafgan laughed mockingly. "Rage away, you hateful bastard! Curse me for all time as you did those below, for I am now among their number! I am an Apostate!"

There was a heartbeat of silence, followed by a low rumbling. Seanai peered outside. Frequent flashes of lightning illuminated the cove.

"Jhullah-Jhulku!" she gasped.

The waters were being pulled back as one would draw back a bow. A massive wave reared ever higher. Within moments the cove was emptied and flashes of lightning revealed the towers and minarets of the sunken city. The wave reared impossibly high.

The lightning flashed again and Seanai beheld a shadow in the frothing white crest of the gigantic wave, a shape which reclined among the churning waters like an infernal emperor upon a throne of stars. From its gaze spilled a cosmic loathing so profound the deepest hatreds of mankind were made childishly trivial. This cosmic abhorrence washed over her, befouling her soul and mangling her reason.

Whimpering like a whipped cur, Seanai tore her eyes away and croaked, "Hermit! Come!"

"No," he said. "I will stand in defiance of Nuada! Flee, Seanai of Ibak, may your gods protect you!"

The Ibakeen did not argue, she leapt down to the first floor parlor, landing in a crouch and the Apostates hemmed her in. They would have crushed her but in desperation Seanai cried, "Why aid your tormentor?"

There was hesitation in those lifeless eyes then, slowly, the circle of warriors parted.

Beyond the walls, the wave built to a deafening roar. Seanai had just seconds. She raced to the casket and threw open the hatch. The inside was lined with thick hides and sealed with tar. Three benches spanned the interior, in the fashion of a rowboat. Seanai scrambled through the opening and secured the hatch with a system of bolts, sealing out the light.

She huddled in the casket, gripping one of the benches. The roar outside reached a crescendo, then her world turned on end. There was the discordant, dizzying sensation of vertigo as the craft was hurled about by like a child's toy. Joints creaked and wood splintered. Something heavy crashed into the outer hull. Seanai felt cold water against her cheek and feared the hull would give way. She was buffeted mercilessly. The casket lurched and she lost her grip. She went tumbling, her skull cracked a strut and she sank into a deep dark oblivion.

From a dream of stalking blind albino Takkel birds among sunless crags, Seanai awoke. She was sprawled in the bottom of the casket and a hand's width of seawater pooled around her. The whole top of the casket had been torn away and sunlight filtered down through the boughs of an oak tree. Birds perched in the branches, singing to each other.

Seanai tried to rise and the casket lurched to one side. She grasped hold of a twisted bench and watched loose timbers fall to the forest floor.

"The wave put us in a tree," Seanai observed to no one. "But I live."

She clambered down the gnarled branches of the sprawling oak and once on the ground, walked back toward the cove. The undergrowth had been ravaged by the deluge, smashed and cluttered with debris. Here and there she identified pieces of the villa and its contents. Then she came upon the new shore of the cove; far inland of where it had previously lay. The promontory where the villa stood was now completely submerged.

"Nuada was more thorough this time. I'd wager that's the cliff face where Hafgan had his home."

Seanai stood looking down on the cove. The waters

were calm and gentle waves splashed against the rocks. The Ibakeen recalled what she had seen at the crest of that great wave and recounted the sight to the birds chirping happily among the boughs.

"Aye. I saw him sitting in that wall of water ere it fell. A great pale, naked bastard, beard full of seaweed and brows crusted with coral. He looked dead at me. By Jhullah-Jhulku, I'd pluck out my eyes rather than meet his gaze again!"

Seanai spat off the cliff, turned on her heel and plunged into the forest.

The End.

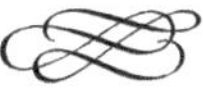

Author Interview with B. Harlan Crawford

Do you remember your first experience with Sword and Sorcery fantasy? Tell us a little about it.

My interest in Fantasy probably began with a viewing of Jason and the Argonauts as a wee lad. My first exposure to Sword and Sorcery proper was through the Marvel Conan comics, which led to me getting the Ace Conan the Warrior paperback. It contained Red Nails and Beyond the Black River. I consider those two stories to be the pinnacle of S&S.

For a long time, publishing companies considered sword and sorcery dead. Now it's making a

comeback. What do you think is responsible for the resurgence of barbarians in loin cloths?

Honestly, I was not aware of this "death" of S&S, likely because there was such a backlog of S&S from the early days I still had to read, I could stay immersed.

As to a resurgence, I'd say the appeal lies in a longing to cast off the yoke of dull, monotonous civilized life, and live as a true, if idealized, savage. Pulp barbarians control their own destiny in a way that many of us cannot.

What draws you to sword and sorcery fiction?

Along with the escapism touched on above, it's the aesthetic of the ancient world with its swords, armor and monolithic structures, filtered through unfettered imagination.

Where do you get your inspiration?

It could be anything; a news story, a trip to the beach, an incident involving friends or family. I find myself thinking along the lines of. "What if this happened to a sorcerer or a barbarian?" "What if this prehistoric creature had survived until the Bronze Age? "What would this become in ten thousand years?"

.   .   .

How long have you been writing and is this your first time in print?

About twelve years. I have previously seen print in two anthologies, and I have self-published a few collections on Kindle Direct. I also put up the occasional story on my blog.

Who is your favorite sword and sorcery author?

For straight Sword and Sorcery my answer can only be Robert E. Howard.

What's your favorite sword and sorcery movie?

The Milius Conan. it was not a perfect adaption, but I felt it captured the spirit of the source material.

I also enjoy Beastmaster quite a bit.

Who made the better Conan? Arnie or Jason Momoa?

Momoa. I'd love to see him get another shot at the role, ideally in a Beyond the Black River adaption.

. . .

What would you like to see more of in future issues of Savage Realms Monthly?

Split skulls, foul sorcery, and ages undreamed of.

How can readers stay in touch with you?

Currently, through my blog:
https://thelibraryoftheschlocklords.blogspot.com/

At some point I might have to create a web page or Facebook account if this writing thing progresses much further.

TITAN'S THRIST

BY ALEXANDER S. KARCHER

SHEETS OF ICE and stinging rain whipped horizontally, scouring the crags rising above the storm-lashed woodlands below. The furious skies roared at the silent earth, and lightning staggered downwards to close the gap. Lluer was angry, and the elements expressed his transcendent rage fully and without reservation.

The wise among the Ullyri knew that to brave the Wilderbrother's wrath would be to risk life and limb and sanity, but the hunter did not consider himself wise. The pious of the tribes preferred communing with the Lord of Beast and Briar during seasons of relative calm, that is any season in which the mighty wind is reduced to a pitiful breeze and the bolts of fire hurtling from the heavens are naught but fading memories of more tempestuous times. The hunter did not think of himself as being an especially pious individual.

Only madmen roamed this part of the world openly during the Riastrad, the yearly bouts of divine madness suffered by the Forest King, Lluer. It was and always had been a time of unprovoked calamity for all residing in or passing through Lluerfen, his vast arboreal domain. Only madmen survived the ire of the god gone mad, and Thedwyr the Hunter had lived in the shadow of madness all his life.

The fading edge of sanity called to him, a voice from the past, a siren's song of days gone by, urgently beckoning him home. He hummed his own discordant jumble of notes, more bestial growl than music, an instinctive acknowledgment and casual evasion of the traps the mind sets for itself. Thedwyr clung to madness like he clung to the jutting shards of cragwall rising before him, the tempest raging at his back, elements frantically beating his half-naked body, and yet held himself apart from it, using it, pushing himself ever upward, higher towards his query.

The man-eater was close.

Thedwyr grunted as he hoisted himself up over the edge of the cliff. He crouched low, steadying his breathing and gathering what remained of his strength. The stone was slick with rain and his body ached from the exertion. The howling wind tore at his waterlogged cloak and plucked at his sodden beard and hair with fingers so cold they burned, teasing him slowly backwards, back towards the edge. The hunter hunkered lower and peered into the swirling madness. There before him, a gash in the rockface-opening into a far deeper darkness than the dark of the storm, was the yawning mouth of the creature's lair.

A fork of lightning cast all before him in an ephemeral light and the momentary vision branded itself onto his mind.

The cave was shallow, its entirety revealed in the one flash of lightning. But it was the cave's denizen, not the cave itself that held the hunter's attention. There at the threshold of the hollow, where earth and storm meet, stood the Beast. He was old, blacker than midnight, wearing the form of a lion, and even the bold stroke of lightning could only illumine the cave he stood in. The beast himself remained a shadow made flesh. His sopping mane dragged the ground, as he tossed its head to and fro, a lazy attempt to shake the water out. It would have been a pitiful sight, if not for his size. The beast was the size of a warhorse, making the cave look small by comparison. Thedwyr took all this in as the sky flashed, then, as darkness returned, the lion was enveloped once more in night, as if he had never been. The only testament to his presence there in the mouth of the cave, were two golden points of light gazing out from the abyss. Intelligent. Calculating.

Thedwyr of the Cathal had found his query. Thunder roared again.

Breathing as softly as he dared, the hunter remained motionless, frozen, not by the cold, but by necessity and purpose.

His heartbeat thundered inside his chest, it seemed to be in direct competition with the raging skies and the rumbling earth.

Focusing his senses, the hunter realized the low rumble from the earth, was not of the earth, but rather the beast at the threshold.

The lion had seen him, and was warning him. He could almost hear it speaking to him. *Be gone manling!*

Thedwyr gently and quietly drew a spear from the clutch he carried on his back.

For a moment which seemed to stretch into eternity, the hunter exhaled. The rain no longer stung as it lashed his face and body, and the deadly chill no longer bit to the bone. In the secret part of him that yet dreamed, madness remained, softly whispering. Madness would never abandon him.

Then the heavens blazed with fire, and bathed the world in white light.

The madman charged. The lion roared and moved to meet his attacker out on the shelf. Darkness returned and drowned the world, yet neither creature stumbled.

The hunter, rushing in, hurled his spear, pulled a second and threw again. The lion reared up and swatted the first away. The second glanced off the his hide. In answer to the hunter's challenge, the lion sprang forwards to close the final distance between the two, claws extended, golden eyes burning. Thedwyr threw himself to the side as the great beast landed where he had been only a moment before. Thunder peeled again in the high places.

Thedwyr, rolled to his feet, third and final spear in hand, and lunged towards the lion's unprotected back; but the old brute, a veteran of many struggles, guessed his intentions, and moved with a speed that belied his size, unnaturally swift, to turn and face his foe. The spear buried itself to the haft in the lion's flank, then snapped in two. Thedwyr stumbled against the beast. The lion's roar seemed to shake the very earth, and its claws raked at the hunter's back. Thedwyr spun, crying out in pain and landed on the ground. He could smell blood in the air.

So too could the man-eater.

The lion rushed the prone hunter, clawing at his legs, raking his chest and arms. Thedwyr yelling, fended off the blows aim at his head with his own thick forearms. Lightning once more turned night into day, and by the light of the storm's fury, Thedwyr looked into the beast's eyes and saw only blackness. The golden light was gone. Be it the scent of blood or the rage of battle, the black slits of the creature's pupils had become engorged and now claimed the eyes entirely as portals into the pitch. Thedwyr, savaged and bleeding, looked into those eyes and recognized his own madness, the Titan's Thirst.

The whispers haunting his mind since his youth, now burst to the fore, revealing the terrible door and he entered, and his body shook. A strength took him, and power rose up in him, and he seized the creature by the throat and somehow rose to his feet, and by sheer brute strength, walked the rearing creature to the edge. Roaring as the Forest King himself, he lifted the old lion on high. Thunder boomed in answer to his offering, and the wind swirled and moaned in anticipation.

Thedwyr, he who was still the hunter, somewhere removed at the back of his own mind, saw the lion staring down at him. Sad golden eyes under heavy lids, as if the creature had been just woken from a restful slumber to which he would shortly return. Thedwyr, he who was not the hunter, but something else, saw only black pits opening onto the void, his own power suddenly rendered meaningless before absolute emptiness. Fire streaked earthwards and lit the world while the eyes remained empty. In terror and rage, Thedwyr who was not Thedwyr at all, but something else, with one cruel hand tore out the old lion's throat, and with the other held the beast aloft a moment while hot blood gushed over his arm and shoulder and chest, and life left the creature, and only then did he let the great beast slump to the ground at the edge of the cliff.

Madness reigned in his mind. The whispering voices roared. The sky shook. Mountains seemed to melt and flow, and the forest followed, and the world, bleeding away into emptiness, and he that was Thedwyr, and not

Thedwyr, stood and laughed at it all, and the laughter was pregnant with terror.

Gradually the power which gripped his mind and enervated his body faded. Racked by pain and exhaustion, Thedwyr the Hunter, of the tribe of Cathal, of the Ullyri nation, fell to his knees next to the body of his enemy. The darkness had returned, yet in sheer magnitude it had been lessened immensely. The storm had departed, broken apart by its own fury. Dawn approached and the sky was clearing, and in the heavens above, populating the vastness, stars yet gleamed, untouched by madness or despair.

The hunter bowed his head, eyes resting upon the slain Lion of Lluer, primal guardian of the Ullyri peoples, and his heart sank. So few of the magnificent beasts remained. As Thedwyr examined it closely, he began to weep, for he knew this lion was not the man-eater. No, the black lion he had stalked for days since the brutal killings at Wodren's Crossroads had been a coward. It had suffered a multitude of blows, leaving enough scars to identify it. This poor old beast had faced every fight it had been a part of head-on, and survived all of them, until this one. Thedwyr had slain a true lord of the crags, and an innocent one at that.

It would be fitting, if he took and wore the pelt of the mighty beast as a mark of his crime. All would know his shame.

Several hours later, Thedwyr stood above a newly built cairn before the cave entrance, black lion pelt hung over his shoulder, and savored the remarkable tranquility that had descended upon the mountains. The afternoon sun shone high above, blanketing Lluerfen and the

Heartmounts in a cozy warmth typical of late spring. The wind, barely tinged with frost, rose often enough as to hinder the warmth from becoming an oppressive heat.

Out of the corner of his eye Thedwyr spied sudden movement. A black shape leaping from one craggy shelf to another. It was the man-eater. The beast stared back at him with pitch black eyes. As Thedwyr watched, it bounded down the crag-wall and towards the forest floor, and Thedwyr became more aware of a growing susurration of voices, whispers at the back of his skull, all speaking to him, calling to him. Madness remained.

The hunter hurried after his query, down from the Heartmounts, towards the small hamlet of Songfell, while the storm gathered inside him once more.

Author Interview with Alexander S Karcher

Do you remember your first experience with Sword and Sorcery fantasy? Tell us a little about it.

This is going to sound like I am trying to be clever but I mean it in all honesty, my first experience with this sort of fantasy was the imaginative play I would come up with as a child. Before I could even read English, much less write anything decipherable, I was running around slaying vile beasts and evil wizards armed only with my enchanted sword masquerading for those without a different sight as a somewhat wieldy stick. I'm not going to claim these personal adventures were brought into existence ex nihilo, but as to the particularities which inspired them I cannot recall. I do recall however the thrill of make-believe battle.

· · ·

For a long time, publishing companies considered sword and sorcery dead. Now it's making a comeback. What do you think is responsible for the resurgence of barbarians in loin cloths?

I could go on about the fall of empires and the tiredness of "civilization" and the desire for the simpler conflicts of an age-that-never-was, but I really think we have Dungeons and Dragons to thank. The archetype seems to be fundamental, it is good to have ways of re-encountering it.

What draws you to sword and sorcery fiction?

A desire to discover new worlds, to meet new peoples and cultures, to share in new adventures, to understand old truths in new ways, that underlying curiosity which attracts me to all fantasy fiction is at the heart of it. Speaking to this sub-genre in particular however I would say it is the low-stakes conflict. Not every bar-fight has to determine the fate of the cosmos, sometimes a character is just trying to survive.

Where do you get your inspiration?

This depends on what is being inspired. Our own histories and mythologies and my personal travels inspire world-building while the movements of my soul and heart tend to inspire poetry. Interesting people, both real and imagined, inspire various characters. Hearing a good story will inspire my giving a semblance of life to a new one. Ultimately, one may trace the chain of inspiration back to a primal cause, let's say the spark of intelligent life in the very beginning and the birth of the imagination, the god-like ability to create something from seemingly nothing. I like to believe that it is an underlying sense of gratitude for being that enables us to bring things forth. I am reminded of the Vala, Aule, from Tolkien's Mythos, and the creation of the dwarves.

How long have you been writing and is this your first time in print?

I have been writing fantasy since middle-school, so about two-decades now. I have published poetry but this is definitely my first work of fantasy fiction to be published.

Who is your favorite sword and sorcery author?

Andrzej Sapkowski. Steven Erikson. Miles Cameron. I am not exactly sure who counts and who doesn't. Whoever first told the story about Samson in the Book of Judges! Nothing quite beats the jaw-bone of a donkey when you are outnumbered a hundred to one.

What's your favorite sword and sorcery movie?

· · ·

Arnold's 1982 Conan the Barbarian. That voice is the quintessential barbarian voice now. Which is ironic considering Austria's historical reign as the omphalos of European culture and civilization for quite a number of years.

Who made the better Conan? Arnie or Jason Momoa?

I grew my hair out for Momoa's Conan but I choose Arnie. See above for reasons.

What would you like to see more of in future issues of Savage Realms Monthly?

More of the same and more of the different. Keep up the good work.

Lastly, how can readers stay in touch with you?

By reading my work.

EYE OF THE SERPENT

BY WILLARD BLACK

NATALI FOLLOWED the big barbarian up a broad and winding stair carved in steep stone, past a gatehouse manned by sleepy guards, to a wide flat plateau ringed by houses cut in ebon rock. The sun was setting and the shadows stretched long. Tehette was an ancient city of basalt towers perched atop green hills rising from the land like arthritic fingers. The people of Tehette did not know who had originally built their vast metropolis. Many ages of man had come and gone since the foundations of the city were laid and the history was all but forgotten. The people who dwelled here now were known as Tehettish, but in fact they were distant cousins of Tanthus far to the south.

Natali mounted the last of the steps and palmed sweat from her forehead. She was a slip of a girl with raven hair, tan skin, and a gold ring in one delicate nostril. She bent over, braced her hands on her knees, and gasped for breath. She was dressed in a tunic several sizes too large, taken from a dead Ashurian and splashed with dried blood. Her spindly legs trembled like a new born colt and dark hair fell down around her shoulders in tangled curtains. "I confess I am not accustomed to such strenuous activity."

They had entered a marketplace of twisting lanes, where street vendors sold everything from livestock and fresh fruit to slaves and finely worked blades.

Redgar snorted. He was a broad shouldered barbarian from the north with blonde hair and muscled limbs. A gigantic blade of steel was balanced on his shoulder. The weapon was nearly as tall as the man who wielded it and worked with eldritch runes. "Were there no stairs in your monastery, Priestess?"

"I'm no priestess," Natali told him with a hint of aggravation. "And, yes, there were stairs."

She turned and gazed back down the steps to the rolling countryside far below. From this height she could see all the land for many miles in every direction and she said, "There weren't *that* many stairs."

"Was there ale?" Redgar asked.

She fixed him with a hard stare. "There was no ale. Nor wine, nor grog, nor beer."

"What did you do for fun?" Redgar asked.

"We devoted our time to study," Natali told him.

"I'd rather have my toenails plucked out by an angry Mai Nu." Redgar took her by the arm and steered her into the crowd. They passed an Ashurian slaver selling Keshite captives. A line of dark skinned savages stood with their heads bowed and their hands clasped in iron shackles. The rotund Ashurian called over the heads of the crowd in a hoarse voice, "Barbarian! Wish you to sell the young wench? I'll give you a king's ransom for such a choice morsel."

"She is not for sale," Redgar called back.

Natali looked on the captives and her brow knotted. "What a foul practice."

"I shouldn't think you would object to the sale of Keshites," said Redgar. "Only last night some of those same savages meant to sacrifice you to their mountain god."

"No one deserves to live in captivity," said Natali. "It is barbarous and evil."

"You say those words like they belong together."

"I did not say that all barbarians were evil, if that is what you mean."

A smile spread across his face and he swept the wild mane back from his forehead. "Civilized men sell one another and call Hathors barbarous, yet Hathor tribes do not keep slaves. Who then are the barbarians?"

Natali pressed her lips together in a tight line. Her delicate nostrils flared. After a moment she said, "I disapprove of the practice no matter which peoples or nations commit such heinous acts."

"You are young and not yet wise to the ways of the world," Redgar said. He led her across narrow arches of stone and creaking bridges of rope and timber spanning the black hills of Tehette, toward the bustling heart of the city suspended high above the countryside.

"I am old enough and wise enough to know we should not be plodding through the town square while Ivashek and his men are searching for us," Natali said and then corrected herself. "For me. I need to reach Vindylhiem in the north. You agreed to take me. We should be on our way."

"I agreed to no such thing," Redgar said. "I said we could make many miles before the sun set and we have done that."

Vindylheim is many months to the north," Natali said with a note of panic in her voice. "I cannot travel so many miles with Ivashek and his men dogging my steps. I would never make it on my own. I need someone to protect me."

"And I need food and drink," said Redgar.

He found a stall selling spits of beef roasting over an open fire. Redgar bought two from a fat man with a mouth full of crooked yellow teeth. He passed one to Natali and the aroma made her mouth water.

It had been three days since she had anything to eat and her stomach grumbled, but her vows forbid her from eating the flesh of an animal. She took the wooden spit in one hand and frowned at the hunk of meat. Greasy fat dripped around her bare feet. Redgar ripped off a hunk of meat with his teeth and chewed while he waited to see how long it would take her to give in. Her face curled in disgust, but her stomach won out. She was dizzy with hunger. If she did not eat soon she would starve. She took a tentative bite, and another, then she set on the fatty slice of beef with all the abandon of a wolf ripping apart prey.

Redgar guffawed. "Come. Let us find a tavern where we can wash down our banquet."

But a spectacle of strength found them first. As they made their way through the crowds, Redgar spotted a raised platform where a man was preparing to do battle with a hairy ape from the jungles of Kesh. The crowd cheered the man as he stepped into the ring. It was no contest. The gorilla tangled with the man and they went down in flurry of limbs. The ape mounted the struggling fighter and rained down fists on the man's unprotected head. Hairy knuckles made sharp cracking noises. Within seconds the fight was over and the man lay in a bloody heap, but the monkey went on hammering at him. The creature's blood was up. It threw back its head and howled as it pummeled the defeated man.

A well-dressed Tehettish gentleman leapt to the edge of the stage and barked a command in some foreign tongue. It was the only thing that kept the ape from bludgeoning the unconscious man to death. The ape raised both arms in victory, working the imitation of a smile onto its ugly flat face.

The crowd booed, but the ape didn't seem to mind.

The vanquished fighter had to be carried off while the well-dressed Tehettish gentleman called out to the crowd. "Who is strong enough, who is brave enough, to face the mighty ape of the Keshite jungles? Fifty gold sovereigns to any man who can tame the beast! Fifty gold! Is there any man among you?"

Redgar tore the last of the meat from the spit and tossed the skewer over his shoulder before calling out, "I shall tame the beast!"

Natali dropped her skewer and latched onto the Hathor's muscular forearm. The food was forgotten and her hunger was replaced by sheer panic. She dreaded to think what would happen to her when the gorilla ripped the Hathor limb from limb. She would be alone in this bizarre city full of extraordinary customs. She held onto his forearm and said, "Are you mad?"

"Relax," Redgar told her, as if battling an ape were an everyday occurrence.

"Relax?" Natali stammered. "Did you see what that beast did to the other man?"

The beaten man was carried past them at that very

moment as if to punctuate her words. His head had swollen up like a pumpkin and he left a trail of blood in his wake.

"Fifty gold sovereign if I win," Redgar said.

"And if you lose?"

Redgar calmly pulled his arm free and said, "You will need to hire yourself another protector."

The Tehettish master of spectacle yelled to be heard over the raucous din. "The barbarian versus the beast! Who will win? Place your bets! Place your bets!"

Natali said, "You cannot possibly beat an animal like that. It will kill you."

He slipped the purse, heavy with coin, from his wide leather belt and handed it to her. "Put twenty gold on me."

"This is madness," Natali told him, "Madness!"

But the barbarian was already cutting through the crowd, leaving Natali alone with the purse. Several spectators slapped him on the back. One woman darted forward to clutch at his broad chest. She grinned like a jungle cat and licked her lips. Redgar hauled himself onto the platform and handed his massive sword to the master of ceremony. The Tehettish man reached for the weapon and the weight of it nearly bowled him over. His eyes opened wide at the size of the blade.

Redgar swung over the frayed ropes into the ring with the grace of a leopard stalking his prey.

"Place your bets!" The master of ceremony called. "Place your bets!"

Natali felt the purse in her hand, heavy with Ivashek's gold, and thought about abandoning the Hathor to his fate. She'd suspected she had fallen in with a ruffian and a drunk. Now she was certain of it. The gold would buy her passage to Sukkali, perhaps as far as Ashur. But who would protect her upon the road? She glanced about the crowd. Lined and swarthy faces surrounded her. For better or worse, the barbarian was her sole defense against this dark and confusing world.

Redgar turned to the crowd and pumped both fists in the air. Powerful muscles rippled beneath his skin. He was met by applause and a few jeers. He turned his attention on the hulking black form of the ape sitting calmly in the center of the ring. The mindless brute watched Redgar with malice in its beady black eyes.

Natali's heart crowded up into her throat and her stomach twisted. She felt she had better place his bet, even if it was a foolish thing to do. It was, after all, his money. She pushed her way through the throng of spectators to a wizened old Suk taking bets. He grinned down at her with a mouthful of gold teeth. "Your savage friend will die in that ring, girlie."

"He'll not die," Natali said with more confidence than she felt. She thrust her chin in the air. "I've seen him best a hundred Keshites in armed combat."

The Suk wheezed out a laugh. "Place your bet then."

Natali counted out twenty gold coin from the purse, then put ten back. If the Hathor lost she would need money for the long road ahead. "Ten gold on the Hathor."

The master of ceremony waved a hand in the air and hollered, "Let the games begin!"

Natali tied the leather purse to the draw strings of the oversize tunic and then stood on her tip-toes in an effort to see above the crowd. Her stomach was a knot of coiling serpents and she felt like she would vomit up the beef.

Redgar waded forward to meet his opponent. The great beast rose from its haunches and spread long, hairy arms layered in muscle, like he was expecting a hug.

Redgar wasn't foolish enough to grapple the ape. He dodged to the outside, clutched at the animal's wrist and hammered a fist down on the beast's elbow. There was a meaty snap and the ape's hairy arm bent the wrong way. A mighty cheer went up from the crowd.

The gorilla bellowed in rage and swung his good arm in a wide arc, catching Redgar a blow on the cheek. The Hathor stumbled back against the ropes, dazed by the attack. The ape was on him in a flash. With a bestial roar, the ape bore Redgar to the platform and raised one hairy fist overhead to pummel the barbarian.

Natali covered her mouth with both hands. For one hopeful moment she had thought Redgar might actually beat the monkey. Now it looked all but hopeless. Natali's heart crawled up into her throat.

Redgar's hands shot out like twin cobras and he clapped his open palms against the ape's ears with a flat *thwack*! The gorilla reared back and fell. It let out a painfilled screeching noise and blundered around the ring. A stunned hush fell over the crowd as the wounded animal stumbled and shrieked.

Redgar leap to his feet, grasped a fistful of the ape's hair and drove his knuckles into the animal's eye socket with a hard crack that split the silence like thunder. He landed two more blows before the ape swatted him away with one vicious swipe of that musclebound arm. Redgar stumbled back but kept his feet. His body was lathered in sweat and a large purple welt was rising on his chin where the ape had cuffed him. He lunged forward, clasped both hands together and brought them down on the beast's head.

While the Hathor battled the ape from the dark jungles of Kesh, Natali noticed a pale skinned woman watching the scene from an open doorway. She was hauntingly beautiful with a lithe body and dark, foreign eyes. The woman studied Redgar with a cold, calculating gaze. Something about her made Natali's skin crawl. As if sensing she was being watched, the woman turned her gaze on Natali.

Gooseflesh marched up Natali's arms in ranks. She quickly looked away, turning her attention back to the fight in time to see Redgar deliver a devastating blow that knocked the wounded ape to the ground in a bloodied heap.

The master of ceremony stood with a dumbfounded expression on his face. The battle was over and his ape had lost. He didn't know what to do. This had never happened before. Redgar stepped to the edge of the stage and pumped both fists in the air to wild applause.

Natali suddenly wished she had put every last gold coin on the Hathor. She would have made enough to hire a dozen strong men to escort her north. She reached down and felt around on the course tunic, but the purse was gone.

By midnight, Redgar was deep in his cups. His ability to quaff wine seemed matched only by his skill in battle. He had been furious to learn Natali had lost the purse and even more angry when he found out she had only placed ten gold on him. The fifty he won from beating the ape helped calm his temper and after collecting his winnings, Redgar had steered a course to the nearest ale house. That was several hours ago. Night had fallen. The sky beyond the narrow slits that served as windows showed a velvet sky dotted with winking diamonds. A thick layer of smoke hung in the air and flickering lamps were suspended overhead, creating halos in the slowly eddying haze. The crowd, most of them witnesses to the fight, were bellowing their way through a Tehettish war chant. Redgar reclined on a low settee, a cup of wine in one bloodied fist, singing along with the mob.

Natali sat on the floor at Redgar's feet, her knees drawn up to her chest and her head pounding from all the raucous laughter and singing. Redgar had toasted admirers and told stories of his adventures while Natali sipped from a cup of stale wine. It was getting late and she longed for a soft pallet. She couldn't remember the last time she had slept. Fate, it seemed, had other plans. She waited for a break in all the reverie and whispered in Redgar's ear. "We should be away from this place. Surely, if Ivashek is in Tehette, he has heard a Hathor bested the ape and will connect it with you."

"*If* he is in Tehette," Redgar said. "He might have ridden east or south."

Natali set her cup down on the flagstone floor and grasped Redgar's thick forearm with both of her small hands. "He rode north, and you know it."

Redgar downed the last of his wine and moped his chin with the back of one hand. An angry purple welt was growing on his jaw. "It is too dark to travel. We shall leave at first light."

"I cannot fall into Ivashek's clutches," she told him. "He would…"

"He would what?" Redgar asked. His eyes cleared and his face sharpened, like he had shrugged off the effects of the alcohol by sheer force of will.

"You could not possibly understand," she told him.

He grunted.

"See me safely to the monastery in Ashur and my order will richly reward you."

"How richly?" Redgar asked.

"Far more than you made fighting an ape with your bare hands," said Natali. "And much less dangerous."

Redgar grinned. "We are far safer indoors than we would be in the wilderness. We'll take rooms here for the night. Ivashek and his sellswords will not try to waylay us with all these witnesses about."

Natali was about to protest when a Keshite rapped his drum and the room fell silent. A dancer, dressed in a simple loincloth hung with silver bells, climbed onto a tabletop; the very same woman Natali had noticed earlier. Her hips undulated to the rhythm of the drums and the tiny bells filled the air with a shrill ring. The Hathor eyed the dancer with open admiration and a terrible sense of foreboding settled over Natali.

The woman made her way across the room until she was dancing in front of Redgar. The Hathor's eyes fixed on her heaving breasts and swaying hips. He watched her dance to the rhythm of the drums and Natali watched the crowd, expecting some evil plot.

When the music ended, the dancer threw herself down on Redgar's lap and arched her back like a jungle cat. The roomful of men cheered. The dancer's eyes flashed across Natali and settled on Redgar. The fingers of her right hand trailed across his broad chest and she smiled. "You are the one who bested the ape."

"You were the one watching me from the doorway," Redgar said.

Natali sat up a little straighter. Redgar had spied the

pale-skinned seductress even as he wrestled the gorilla, perhaps he was not nearly as dumb as Natali believed?

The woman nuzzled Redgar's ear with her nose and asked, "What is a Hathor doing in Tehette with a Rhaji girl barely old enough to bleed?"

Natali bristled.

"I could ask you the same," Redgar said. "You are not Tehettish. From where did you come?"

"Utali, west of the Scorching Wastes," she purred. Her fingers trailed down Redgar's chest to his muscled stomach. "I've never met a Hathor man before. Utali women whisper terrible tales of the savages from beyond the Frost Gate." Her fingers found the top of his wide leather belt and she said, "Are the rumors true?"

"There is but one way to find out," Redgar told her.

Natali had a pillow over her head and her eyes shut tight, trying to block out the sounds coming from the next room. Redgar was grunting and the Utali woman shrieked. Their frenzied noises penetrated the walls.

It reminded Natali of the terrible spectacle she had witnessed as a captive of the savage Keshites. Only this was different. These were not screams of terror and violation. Instead of pain, the Utali woman moaned with undisguised pleasure. And though Natali loathed the pale-skinned seductress, the urgent moaning awakened something deep within Natali.

She laid there trying to block out the noise but curiosity got the better of her. She threw off the pillow and sat up. The room was a simple affair, just a sleeping pallet and a wash stand in one corner. Moonlight filtered in through a single window, carrying with it a whiff of piss and stale beer from the alley below. Natali crept to the door, eased down on the rusting latch, and winced at the creak of aging hinges. She stepped into the darkened upstairs hall and went on bare feet to Redgar's room.

A light burned within. Natali found a small crack in the rough timbers, put her eye to the opening and let out a small gasp. Her heart seized within her chest even as a fire ignited in her belly.

By the gods! It was like the Keshites, and yet it wasn't.

Through the narrow gap Natali glimpsed two bodies entwined together, lathered in sweat, grasping and pawing. "Harder," the Utali woman cried. Her face turned and, for a moment, Natali was sure the women looked right at her, like she knew Natali was standing on the other side of the door. Something wicked flashed in those dark eyes. A knowing smile spread across her lips. "Harder, you brute!"

Natali fled back to her own chamber where she curled up on the pallet with her face to the wall. She had seen enough. Too much. She was both disgusted and enthralled. She pulled the pillow over her head, closed her eyes, and tried to ignore a wet heat between her legs.

When it was over, Redgar lay with his head propped on his arm. The Utali woman rested her cheek on his chest. Her fingertips traced the lines of his tummy. He said, "Now perhaps you'll tell me what you wish of me."

All the warmth drained from her face. What remained was cold, calculating beauty.

Redgar said, "An exotic jewel like you could have any man she wanted. A rich Noble or the hand of the king even. I may be a barbarian, but I'm no fool. You want something, woman. Speak."

She draped her body over his and propped her chin on his chest. Her slender fingers grasped his muscular arms. "There is a man in Tehette—a thief—in possession of a rare jewel, a peridot of the finest quality. I desire it."

"Must be the size of a man's head," Redgar commented.

"No bigger than a child's fist," she told him.

"A trinket that size is hardly worth the trouble."

"To you," she said. "To me it is worth more than all the gemstones in all the world."

"And who is this thief?" Redgar asked. "A former accomplice?"

"A simple burglar who took what does not belong to him."

"And you want it back," Redgar said. It was more a statement than a question but she nodded all the same.

"Where would I find this burglar?" Redgar asked. "If I decide to look."

"Tonight he sleeps beneath the roof of a whorehouse in the tanner district."

"The Milk and Thistle," Redgar said. "I know it well."

The Utali woman didn't react to that.

"I don't even know your name," Redgar said.

"Jaira."

"How badly do you want this stone, Jaira?"

She slithered down his belly to his waist, trailing kisses the whole way. "I would do anything to possess it."

~

Redgar found the thief's window easy enough. The Hathor learned the location from a tavern wenche for two gold coin. It was on the second floor above a treacherous drop to a flagstone courtyard, but the carven houses of Tehette made climbing easy work for the barbarian. He scaled the side of the building under the light of a waxing moon and chanced a peek through the open window. The thief lay passed out on a pallet surrounded by four women. Naked limbs glowed in the spill of starlight.

Armed with only a dagger, Redgar slid through the window frame like a shadow and stole across the room to a leather sack at the foot of the bed. He crouched and quietly removed the contents in search of the gemstone. All he found was a thief's toolkit and climbing gear. Redgar frowned, wondering where the precious stone could be hidden in such a tiny chamber.

One of the girls turned in her sleep, moving her arm in the process, and revealing a shining green jewel laying on the thief's chest. The man was wearing it on a silver chain around his neck.

Redgar's face clouded over. No wonder the Utali strumpet needed a warrior instead of a thief. It would take a magician to pluck the stone from the thief's neck unnoticed. Redgar slipped the dagger from his wide belt. He meant to stab the burglar in his sleep and make off with the gemstone before any of the girls saw his face, but the thief's eyes snapped open at the tell-tale whisper of the dagger drawing from its sheath.

With a shout of alarm, the burglar sprang from the sleeping pallet and threw himself at Redgar. A long slim blade appeared in his hand as if by magic. The bastard must have been sleeping with it under his pillow. He slashed and parried, forcing Redgar to retreat across the room.

The girls woke with a freight, laid eyes on the giant barbarian bathed in moonlight, and loosed shrieks that would wake the whole house. Redgar had seconds to make his escape before armed guards—hired to protect the ladies—came bursting in.

He provided an opening in his defense and the thief lunged, trying to bury his knife in Redgar's chest. Steel flashed as Redgar swatted the blade aside. He caught the thief's wrist and twisted. The man lost his grip on the weapon and the knife fell to the floor. Redgar could hear boots on the stairs. He dropped his own dagger, caught the thief by the balls and hefted the man into the air. The burglar gave a surprised yelp as Redgar tossed him out the open window.

There was a shriek and then a hard wet smack as the thief landed on the paving stones.

Redgar grasped the edges of the window frame as the door burst open. There was a moment of confusion as two hired thugs shouldered their way into the room and the whores all tried at once to tell them what had happened. One of the sellswords saw Redgar in the window and raised his truncheon. Redgar leapt.

He landed on both feet with a heavy thump. The impact sent a shockwave of pain racing up through his brawny legs. His face pinched, but he had survived the fall and was no worse for wear. The thief was still alive as well, though he had landed flat on his back. He let out a painful moan and twitched his limbs.

Redgar yanked the gemstone from the man's neck with one savage jerk and fled from the courtyard, chased by shouts from the guards. He reached the garden gate and sprinted along a narrow street, not sure where he was going, only that he needed to put as much distance between himself and the whore house as possible. He turned a corner and ran headlong into a pack of armed men.

Natali came awake with a start, a scream dying on her lips. Her heart was thudding inside her chest and gooseflesh marched up her arms in ranks. She had been dreaming of brightly lit chambers deep beneath the earth and beds with glass coverings connected to living fire. At first she thought the nightmare had woken her, then her sleep clouded mind registered the form of a man slipping in through the open window.

She tried to summon up a scream but the shadowy apparition was on her before Natali could draw breath. A hand clamped over her mouth and she heard him say, "Hush child! You'll wake the whole house."

Natali grasped at a muscle bound forearm, trying in vain to pull his hand away. It was another moment before she realized it was Redgar and that he was hurt. He gripped her tight until her struggles subsided. "I'm going to let you go," he told her. "Do *not* scream."

He took his hand away and Natali gasped for breath. She felt like she had just escaped an iron manacle. She said, "What are you doing sneaking around in the night like a common criminal?"

"Criminal acts," Redgar told her as if that should be obvious. His voice was hoarse and Natali sensed more than saw blood drying on his arms.

"You've been hurt."

He nodded.

Natali threw off the covers and lit a lamp. The flickering flame filled the tiny chamber with a leaping glow that threw grotesque shadows on the wall. Redgar had his back to the window and one hand pressed over a deep gash in his shoulder. The other hand gripped a flashing green stone the size of a child's fist. Blood had dried on his bronze arms and there was a small cut over one eyebrow.

"What happened?" Natali asked.

"I went to retrieve a gemstone for the Utali woman and now half the city is after me."

"I knew that vile woman was trouble," Natali said. She tore a strip of linen from the bedclothes and tied it around the gash on his shoulder. "I tried to warn you."

"I should have listened," said Redgar. While Natali tended to his wounds, Redgar told her briefly about his adventure ending with, "I was waylaid on my way back here by half a dozen lads armed with short swords. They were all dressed in white robes emblazoned with a crimson insignia upon their breasts. They seemed to be looking for the gemstone as well. I barely escaped."

"You should give that jewel to the Utali seductress straight away and be done with it."

He shook his head. "Not until I know it's worth and why half the brigands in Tehette are after it."

"Even if it costs your life?"

"My life's not worth a wooden penny." Redgar told her as he tied the gemstone on its leather thong around her neck. "Hold onto it for me until I find out why Jaira is so desperate to possess it."

After she had tended his wounds, Redgar sent Natali next door to fetch his sword, then put his head down on the thin pillow and let his eyes slip closed.

A high-pitched shriek yanked the barbarian from sleep. He threw off the covers and sprang to his feet. His powerful legs were bunched and ready to move. He didn't know if he had slept hours or only minutes, but the sky beyond the window was still dark.

There was a commotion in the hall—another muffled scream followed by the sounds of a struggle. Redgar went to the door, poked his head into the corridor, and pulled back in time to avoid an arrow. The missile buried itself in the wood frame with a solid *thock!*

Redgar had glimpsed Natali wrestling against four brigands dressed in black. She had been on her way back from fetching his sword and tried to defend herself with it, but the massive blade was too heavy for her to lift, let alone swing.

Redgar chanced another peek.

One of the assassins pulled back on a curved short bow and released. Another arrow embedded itself in the doorframe. Leaving the room would be instant death. He could only wait while the brigands bound the struggling girl and look for an opportunity.

Ivashek's henchmen or Jaira's? Redgar wondered. Or some other faction intent on claiming the stone? His brow furrowed.

Natali did not give up without a fight. The bandits had to haul her, kicking and shrieking, to the head of the stairs. They tried to take Redgar's sword as well but quickly decided it was too heavy to bother with. One of the thieves gagged Natali as they wrestled her down the steps.

As soon as the upstairs hall was clear, Redgar left the safety of the doorframe and snatched up his weapon on his way to the staircase. The bandits had already reached the bottom and were carrying Natali across the darkened common room by the time Redgar was on the steps. He bounded across the floor, turning over a table in his hurry to catch the brigands but, by the time he stepped into the moonlit street, the boulevard was empty.

The barbarian's sharp ears caught the scuff of hurried feet and he loped along, peering down side streets in search of his prey. He caught sight of the bandits as they turned a corner and sprinted along an empty alleyway strewn with trash. Redgar gave chase through a twisting maze of confusing passages, determined to catch the thieves but instead came to an intersection and found himself face to face with the men in white robes that he had so narrowly escaped earlier.

Redgar drew up short. His face worked into a snarl. He growled, "You again?"

A voice in back of him said, "Us again."

Redgar wheeled around and saw a flash of steel. Something hard impacted his temple and darkness swallowed him whole.

Terror surged through Natali. The cords binding her wrists bit deep into her flesh and her heartbeat sounded like thunder in her ears. She was carried, moaning into the gag, through the streets of Tehette. The whole time she thought she was being taken to Ivashek. But the robed henchmen carried her along dark alleyways to a door cleverly concealed in the basalt rockface behind a large and ominous temple.

Natali doubled her efforts when the secret door sighed

open on unseen hinges to reveal a dark maw like the mouth of some forgotten god. Her struggles were rewarded with a hard slap across the face. Her head rocked to the side and her vision blurred. When it cleared she was being dragged along a dimly lit passage cut in the rock. Her captors carried her down a winding stair to a shadowy throne room dominated by an immense statue of a coiled serpent. The head of the great snake hovered twenty feet above the floor. One eye was a gleaming peridot. The other was an empty cavity, and Natali knew the stone hanging around her neck belonged in that dark hollow.

In the center of the floor, at the foot of the giant snake, was a large open pit. A foul stench wafted from the chasm. Her captors carried Natali around the pit to the base of the reptilian statue. For one terrible moment she thought they were going to hurl her into the stinking abyss.

A shadow detached itself from a dark corner near the altar and the Utali woman strode forward. She was naked save for a slender belt of silver holding up an emerald sash that trailed the floor. A hungry light danced in her dark eyes as she crossed the chamber to stand in front of Natali. She arched a carefully sculpted brow and asked, "Why have you brought me the youth?"

"She possesses the stone, Priestess." One of the henchmen yanked open the oversized tunic to reveal the gleaming jewel at the end of its leather thong.

Jaira's eyes lighted on the winking peridot hanging between the small buds of Natali's breasts. She sucked air in through clenched teeth and reached out a hand, but stopped short of touching the gemstone. Instead she caressed the naked flesh around Natali's nipple and spoke in a throaty whisper. "At long last."

Natali was finally able to work the gag from her mouth.

She said, "You may have the stone. I have no use for it. Take it and let me go."

A cruel smile turned up one corner of Jaira's sensuous mouth. "Any who dare touch the Eye of the Serpent must die."

A spasm of fear marched up Natali's spine. Her knees buckled, but one of the henchmen caught her and held her up. He was careful not to touch the stone. She looked about wildly for any kind of help but she was alone in the terrible altar room with the priestess and her minions. Her chin trembled as she said, "Please, just let me go."

Jaira's fingertips trailed up Natali's breastbone leaving a trail of fire in their wake. The priestess traced Natali's brow and said, "Such a waste that one so innocent must die, but I'm not without mercy. Carry out a simple task for me and I will make your death quick."

Natali started to shake her head.

The priestess caught her chin in a powerful grip. "Refuse and my worshippers will strip the skin from your bones in tiny ribbons. You will beg for death before the end!"

Natali's heart trembled within her chest. She licked dry lips and asked, "What must I do?"

Jaira turned her eyes up to the looming head of the snake. "Place the eye in the serpent's head and your death will be painless. I promise."

A henchman cut Natali's bonds with a dagger and gave her a push toward the statue. She stumbled but managed to keep her feet. Jaira's followers fanned out to block the exit. The only other escape was to throw herself into the pit. Tears trailed down Natali's cheeks as she put one bare foot on the base of the coiled serpent and pulled herself onto the body of the effigy. She forced herself to mount the coils. The stone was cold and clammy beneath her hands. She felt almost that she was climbing a live snake. Twice she almost fell and was forced to hug the thick body of the serpent as she scrambled toward the head. She could see down into the pit from here and at the bottom she glimpsed brackish green ooze. She reached the head, lifted the leather thong over her head and paused.

"Do it!" Jaira hissed. The priestess stood directly beneath the serpent's gapping maw, her naked chest heaving in anticipation. Her voice shook with passion. "Replace the eye!"

Natali thought about hurling the jewel into the pit, but that would not help her predicament. Jaira's henchmen would carve her into ribbons, after they had defiled her no doubt. Better to replace the stone and suffer a quick death.

With shaking fingers, Natali bent over the wedged shaped head of the snake and seated the peridot in the empty eye socket. The stone locked into place with soft click and Natali felt a shudder run through the stone between her legs. The eyes flashed with green light and the throne room filled with a terrible sound that caused Natali's teeth to vibrate in her skull. She clapped both hands over her ears and would have fallen off, but she clamped her legs tight around the humming stone.

Jaira raised both hands in the air and shouted. "Come forth, O great Serpent God of the Realms beyond Time. Come and claim your faithful servant. Come Great Snake! Awaken!"

From the mouth of the statue, a poisonous green serpent emerged. The viper dropped to the stone floor of the chamber with a cold wet plop, landing directly in front of Jaira. She fell to her knees and spread her arms wide in a gesture of surrender. "I am your Priestess, O Serpent God!"

The snake slithered around her knees, up her back and over her shoulder. The long reptile body coiled around her and Natali watched in horror, as the serpent flicked its forked tongue into Jaira's open mouth. The priestess whispered to the snake, offering herself to her serpent god. The snake's head swayed hypnotically in front of Jaira's face for a moment, then slid down between her naked breasts to disappear beneath the simple sash hanging between her thighs. Jaira's eyes opened wide in surprise and horror. She jerked and a blood curdling scream ripped from her lips.

The henchmen dropped their knives and retreated to the corners of the room and Natali knew she should try to escape, this might be her one chance, but she couldn't take her eyes off the horrific spectacle. Jaira was on her back writhing in pain as more and more of the snake disappeared between her thighs. Her screams echoed around the chamber, bouncing off the walls and rebounding until it sounded like the souls of the damned all screaming at once. Natali thought it would drive her mad. She realized she was screaming as well.

Then the snake had vanished and Jaira lay still. Her eyes were open and her naked body lay stretched upon the floor. She looked dead. The acolytes stared in horror at the body of their priestess and Natali decided to make her escape. She clambered down from the stone serpent and sprinted around the pit toward the only exit, her heels hammering the paving stones and her stomach creeping up into her throat.

Jaira sat up and shouted, "Fools! Do not let her escape!"

The henchmen quickly blocked Natali's path. She tried to back track into the chamber, but the acolytes were faster. One of the men wrapped his arms around her waist. Another scooped up a knife and put the blade to her throat. Natali felt the edge press against her exposed skin. Her eyes opened wide and she started to scream.

"Stay your hand," Jaira ordered. Her voice was a sibilant hiss. She rose from the ground and a forked tongue darted between those seductive lips. Her eyes had changed to reptilian slits. She said, "Would you slay the Keeper of the Sacred Flame?"

The acolyte took the knife from Natali's throat.

Natali stared at the snake priestess in disbelief.

Jaira threw back her head and laughed. In that slippery serpent's voice, she hissed, "I know what you are, Ancient Sleeper. Child of Doom."

Redgar was in a low chamber with a single lantern hanging from an exposed beam overhead. Iron shackles bound his wrists and bit into his skin. He flexed his shoulders and jerked at the bonds, but they were securely fastened to an iron ring in the wall.

Three of his captors stood watch at the door. They wore white robes emblazoned with a red poppy upon their breasts and stood with their hands on their sword hilts.

"Who are you?" Redgar demanded.

When they didn't answer he growled, "Unbind me and face me as men, you cowardly dogs!"

They watched him with furrowed brows.

Redgar ranted and raved, rattling his chains and cursing them. When that didn't work he sat quiet and waited in brooding silence. Sometime later the heavy iron door groaned open on rusting hinges and a short squat man with grey in his beard entered. At his side stood a tall, well built youth with hair of flaxen gold. He was the one who had clobbered Redgar.

The bearded man gathered his white robes and crouched in front of Redgar. "You are a Hathor?"

Redgar nodded.

"You are a long way from the Frost Gate," the older man said.

Redgar simply stared at the man. He knew the many leagues to the Frost Gate. He had crossed them, mostly on foot, living by wits and the cut of his blade.

The man said, "What does a barbarian want with the Eye of the Serpent?"

"I know not what you are talking about," Redgar said. "I have no interest in serpents."

"Where is the stone?" the man demanded.

"I haven't got it," Redgar said.

"Who does?" the man asked.

"I don't know."

The young man stepped forward and spoke though clenched teeth. "He lies! Give me ten minutes alone with the brute. I'll beat it out of him."

Redgar chuckled. "You couldn't beat the truth from a besotted whore."

The youth cuffed Redgar across the face. It was a flat, hard smack that turned Redgar's head to the side. It stung but Redgar refused to show any sign of pain, refused to give the young pup the satisfaction. He spat on the flagstone floor instead and glared at the young man with eyes that smoldered.

The older man held up a hand. "Come now,

barbarian. We do not wish to inflict pain. We're not torturers."

Redgar tugged at his chains in response to that.

"Unfortunate, but my brethren assure me quite necessary," The old man said. "They tell me you are something of a rogue and a ruffian."

Redgar barked a laugh. "I am both of those things."

"And yet you claim to have no interest in the stone," he said. "Why did you steal it?"

"I didn't steal it. I stole it back," Redgar told him. "It was taken by a thief and I was asked to retrieve the stone by the lady, Jaira."

The young warrior snarled, "What did the snake priestess promise you, barbarian?"

"She promised me nothing," Redgar said. "She paid handsomely in her own way. You're too young to understand."

The youth stiffened and his ears turned red. "He admits he is in league with the snake worshippers."

"Yes," the older man said. "Which is how I know he speaks the truth."

The young man's eyes bulged from their sockets and his hand tightened on the hilt of his sword.

"Would he admit to such if he knew who Jaira was?" The old man asked. "Or had any idea the significance of the stone?"

The younger man calmed himself with a visible effort.

"The stone is no bigger than the young buck's nut sack," Redgar said, "And probably bigger by far than his prick. Why is everyone so eager to possess it?"

"You ignorant barbarian," the young man snarled. "It is worth far more than you could possibly imagine. Your lust has doomed us all."

The old man ended the angry outburst with a wave of his hand. He turned his attention back to Redgar and said, "Jaira is the high priestess in a cult devoted to the demon serpent known as Set. For hundreds of years, the Setites terrorized Tehette and all the lands far and wide with their dark rituals and human sacrifices. In those days, the Brotherhood of the Sacred Heart was the only thing holding back darkness.

"When I was just a young adept—younger than Brom here is now," he nodded to the younger man, "we raided the temple of Set and I plucked the gemstone from the eye of the great serpent with my own hand. The power of the snake demon was broken and we have spent all those years, from that one to this, guarding the stone here in our stronghold.

"Without the power of their demon lord to guide them, the followers of Set dispersed. Their reign of terror had ended. But a few remain loyal and have spent their time watching and waiting," he continued. "Then, this was three nights ago, a thief penetrated our sacred halls and made off with the Eye of the Serpent. Since then, we have been desperately trying to recover the stone before Jaira and her followers could lay hands on it."

"And if they do?" Redgar asked.

The older man shook his head and a deep unsettling fear stole into his cloudy eyes. "Tehette will fall under the dominion of the Snake."

"Unbind me," Redgar said.

The man looked surprised and taken aback, as if Redgar had asked him to scoop fire into his lap.

Redgar briefly told the Brethren of the Sacred Heart how he had taken the stone from the thief and then how it was stolen, along with Natali, when a group of rogues attacked the Inn. He ended with, "If what you say it true, then the brigands who kidnapped Natali and took the stone work for Jaira. They may even now be resurrecting their dark god. Release me and I'll retrieve the stone from the cultists."

Brom snorted. "Why should we trust you? A barbarian who has already admitted he was a willing servant of the Serpent Priestess?"

"Who will defeat the snake worshippers?" Redgar asked. "You?"

Brom thrust his chin in the air. "I'd give my life for the cause."

"I have no doubt," Redgar said. "But dying on the sword of a cultist will not retrieve the stone or save Natali."

"This girl, Natali," the man said. "What is she to you? Your daughter? Your concubine?"

"She is a scholar of some kind," Redgar told him. "I plucked her from the clutches of Keshite raiders."

"And now you feel responsible for her?"

Redgar shrugged one massive shoulder. "I'd rather not see her sacrificed to a snake."

"Give me your word you will retrieve the Eye of the Serpent."

"On my word as a Hathor, clan of the White Wolves, I will bring back the Eye of the Serpent."

"Release him," the older man said.

One of the brethren stepped forward and took a ring of keys from his belt. He didn't look happy about turning the barbarian loose, but he bent and removed the shackles. Brom's knuckles turned white on his sword hilt and he eyed Redgar warily.

Redgar massaged chaffed wrists.

The older man stuck out a hand. "I am called Kreeger."

Redgar introduced himself and Kreeger said, "Fetch his sword."

The first dim rays of light broke over the eastern horizon, tinging the sky with a soft warm glow. The sun would soon be up and the city would teem with life but for now, the only people awake were street vendors erecting their stalls in silence, and Redgar, followed by a dozen Brethren armed with short swords and clubs. They marched through the streets to the temple of set, rearing above the surrounding houses like a grim reminder of darker days.

They stopped at the steps leading to a stone arch.

"It has been abandoned for years," Brom said.

"Or so you thought," Redgar told him.

The two men had formed an uneasy truce. For the moment, they were fellow soldiers united against a common enemy.

Brom said, "We should look for another entrance. Kreeger said there used to be a secret door in back of the temple."

"By the time we find it the cultists will have finished their dark work," Redgar said. "They may have finished already. Come, let us be about our noble deeds."

He mounted the steps, the giant's sword balanced on his broad shoulder, and paused in front of a set of bronze doors worked with the image of twin serpents. He swung the blade down off his shoulder and laid it on the ground before bracing his hands against the towering doors. The muscles in his arms and legs bulged with the effort and the bronze portals groaned slowly open.

Redgar pushed until he could slip through the gap, then took up his sword and plunged into the dark aperture. The Brothers of the Sacred Heart followed him into a lofty chamber. A thick carpet of dust muffled their footfalls on the stone floor. Redgar led the way across the entry hall. On the far side was a pair of openings. One led to a stair which climbed the tower. The other plunged into the dark depths beneath the temple.

"Up or down?" Redgar asked.

"Down," Brom said without hesitation. "These filthy cultists always do their ugly work in the dark."

Redgar nodded in agreement and took the winding stair deep into the heart of the temple. He found himself in a broad, underground passage rank with the odor of death and decay and followed the hallway until he came to the throne room.

Across the wide chasm, the barbarian beheld the looming statue of the snake with its winking green eyes. Jaira stood at the base of the statue, surrounded by a dozen of her black robed henchmen and she had Natali by the neck. A cruel smile turned up her lips.

Redgar strode into the throne room and swung the sword down off his shoulder. "Let her go!"

Jaira looked up with an angry hiss. Her eyes were dangerous slits. She said, "Kill the intruders!"

The black robed apostles of the snake demon rushed around the yawning chasm with their knives bared and Redgar ran to meet them. Young Brom and the Brethren of the Sacred Heart never hesitated. They met the charging snake worshippers in a clash of steel. Blades flashed and men grunted. The Brotherhood was closely matched by the demon worshippers.

Redgar tipped the scales.

He cut a swath through the black robed figures with heroic swipes of his massive sword. Two of the cultists died under his blade. He caught the first man with a vicious swing that chopped the head from the man's shoulders and sent it bounding across the chamber spilling shocks of red blood. He split the other man down the middle with an overhead chop, like he was cutting wood for a fire. The broad steel blade bit into the man's shoulder and cleaved all the way down through his breastbone. A warm wet spray caught the barbarian in the face. He jerked his weapon free of the sagging corpse and turned, looking for another victim. He was just in time to turn the thrust of a knife and heard Jaira shriek, "Hold! Or the girl dies!"

Everyone stopped and turned at the sound of her voice.

The snake priestess had a fistful of Natali's silky black hair and a curved dagger to her throat.

"Cast down your weapons or I will cut her throat," Jaira commanded in a sibilant hiss.

Redgar hesitated, but let the giant sword fall to the floor with a ring of steel.

The Brotherhood of the Sacred Heart had no such intentions. They held onto their weapons.

Jaira pressed the knife edge until it dimpled Natali's flesh. "I am running out of patience."

Redgar turned to Brom. "Drop your swords."

"We are here to retrieve the stone and put an end to her madness," Brom said. "I care nothing for the girl."

Redgar drove his fist into Brom's belly. The young man doubled over with a cough and his sword slipped from limp fingers. Redgar turned to the others and barked, "Lay down your arms!"

"Traitor," Brom croaked.

Redgar faced the priestess and said, "Let her go."

A smile played over Jaira's lips. She said, "Very well."

She took the knife away from Natali's throat and gave her a push.

Redgar watched the girl stumble to the edge of the pit, wheel her arms for balance, lose the struggle and tumble over the edge with a scream. She disappeared into the wide chasm and her scream was drowned out by a maniacal laugh from Jaira. At the same time, the black robed acolytes of Set hacked into the Brotherhood. Three of the stalwart young fighters died in a flash of steel. Swords bit into unprotected bellies and split skulls. Hot red blood spilled across the floor of the temple in violent sprays.

Young Brom managed to roll free, narrowly avoiding a strike aimed at his neck. He clutched a fallen sword and sprang back to his feet, ready to fight.

Redgar ducked a whistling blade, sprinted to the edge of the pit, and peered over the side. Natali had survived the fall and found a giant serpent coiled at the bottom of the pit. The body of the snake wrapped twice around the base of the pit before disappearing through an open archway. A wedge-shaped head rose from the water and swayed hypnotically in front of the girl. A forked tongue flicked out from its mouth.

Natali opened her mouth to scream but no sound came out. She was horror struck. She backed up against the wall and closed her eyes tight.

Redgar heard movement behind him and spun into a crouch. A sword whistled over his head. He grabbed the snake worshipper by the front of his tunic and carried the man over the edge. The henchman screamed as they fell.

Redgar had been aiming for the snake's bobbing head, but missed and they crashed down in the slimy ooze. Brackish water poured down Redgar's throat, choking him. He pushed himself up for air and spat. The acolyte came up out of the water at the same time, spluttering and gasping for air.

The snake let out a hiss and the wedge-shaped head whipped around to face these new intruders on his domain. The giant serpent had lived in the bowels of the temple for many ages of men, feasting on human sacrifices, but it had been years since the snake tasted flesh. It had been living on rats and smaller snakes, any creature which accidentally found its way into the bowels of the temple. Now, for the first time in decades, it had flesh to feast upon and it could not decide who to eat first.

Redgar wasted no time. He raised one foot and kicked the cultist in the back. The man staggered forward into the snake's path. The ancient beast moved with a speed that defied rational thought. The scaly body wrapped around the cultist and began to squeeze. He gave one horrid shriek as the bones in his body splintered. Dark red blood vomited up from his mouth. The snake hinged open its jaw.

Natali chanced a peek, saw the snake devouring the cultist and screamed in mind numbing horror. The sound was like knives in Redgar's ear. He went down on hands and knees, feeling around the floor of the pit for the cultist's weapon. His fingers closed on something hard. He pulled it up from the ooze only to find a cracked bone. Redgar cast away the grisly artifact and went on searching.

The snake continued to work its jaws around the cultist. He had stopped struggling and everything but his legs had disappeared into the great serpent's mouth. Redgar knew he did not have long to live. When the snake finished with the cultist it would turn on him, or Natali. He felt around the water until his hand happened upon steel.

Redgar lifted the weapon in triumph. It was not the cultist's blade, but an older sword, pitted with rust, and a winking ruby was set in the handle. Redgar wondered how many men had met their doom at the bottom of this pit. The thought flashed through his mind even as he pushed to his feet.

The snake had managed to swallow all but the cultist's twitching feet. Natali threw her hands over her head and curled into a ball. Redgar sprang forward, burying the rusty sword to the hilt in the snake's engorged neck. Dark blood dribbled from the wound. The serpent whipped around in pain and fury. Redgar was thrown aside. He impacted the wall with bone rattling force and slid down into a heap.

The sword had pinned the dead man in the snake's gullet. The beast opened its jaws wide in an attempt to swallow, but the body was stuck. The snake thrashed, whipping this way and that, trying to desperately to disgorge the man but that didn't work either.

Redgar shook his head to regain his senses and pushed up from the ground. He slogged across the watery pit and threw his body over Natali in time to shield her from the writhing serpent. The heavy coils crashed into Redgar and he grunted in pain. Natali whimpered beneath him. He braced himself and took two more savage blows before the snake finally fell into the water with a splash. It wasn't dead, not yet, but its prodigious strength was failing.

Redgar grasped Natali's elbow and pulled her to her feet. "We have to get out of here."

He dragged her across the shallow pool to the open arch. They ducked a low mantle and Redgar had to run bent at the waist. The snake's body filled most of the tunnel. One death spasm and they would be crushed against the sloping wall. Redgar tried not to think about that as he led Natali through tunnel. The snake's body seemed to go on forever. Redgar and Natali splashed through knee deep water, until they passed the snake's twitching tail and found a narrow staircase leading up. The snake would never fit through such a small passage. The pit was its prison as well as its home.

Redgar and Natali took the steps two at a time. Both were soaked in foul smelling water. They came out behind the statue and Redgar motioned Natali to the effigy. "Fetch the eyes from the statue's head," he told her. "And be quick about it. The gemstones give the snake god his power."

Natali was already mounting the coiled body. "I know."

Redgar passed around the base of the statue. He was now in back of Jaira. On the opposite side of the wide chasm, he saw young Brom and three of the Brethren fighting for their lives against a dozen of the black robed cultists. The stalwart Brethren cut and slashed with their blades, hacking limbs and stabbing but the cultists fought on despite mortal wounds. Redgar watched as two of the dead cultists sat up, picked up their swords and rejoined the battle.

Jaira stood with her hands outstretched and her face turned up to the ceiling, chanting strange words in a sibilant hiss. Redgar did not need to know anything about sorcery to know the snake priestess was giving life to her dead servants. Across the chamber, a headless corpse stood up, picked up a sword and hacked one of the Brethren to death.

Redgar glanced around for a weapon but found none close to hand. His own sword was on the other side of the alter room. He would have to circle the pit to fetch it and come back. By that time, Jaira would know he had escaped the depths. He thought about pushing her into the pit but there was nothing to stop her from climbing the same stair he had come up.

The Hathor clasped his hands together, stalked up behind the snake priestess and brought both fists down on her head with a hard crack. Jaira's knees buckled and her words were cut short. As soon as she stopped chanting, the dead cultists sank to the ground.

The priestess spun to face Redgar. Her eyes were reptilian slits and her lips parted in an evil smile. A forked tongue flicked from her open mouth as she hissed, "Lover."

Redgar took a step back and Jaira advanced on him. Her head and shoulders swayed like a coiled viper. Redgar doubted strength alone could overcome such evil. His eyes fell on a sputtering torch in a bracket at the base of the statue. The bottom of the torch was carved into a snake's pointed tail. He jerked it free of the bracket, turned and drove the sharp end through Jaira's naked belly.

The priestess clasped the flaming torch in both hands and cried out in pain. The skin of her belly rippled as if some creature writhed just below the surface. Redgar's eyes opened wide in surprise. He watched Jaira's mouth hinge open and the skin of her cheeks split as she disgorged a poisonous green serpent. Her throat swelled to twice its size and she made gagging noises as the snake wriggled free of her mouth. Her eyes were opened wide in pain and horror.

Redgar stumbled backwards into the statue. He had never seen sorcery like this before and he was transfixed.

Jaira sank to her knees and her eyes rolled up as the snake trailed from her open mouth. When the last of the snake left her body, Jaira fell to the floor. The sputtering torch was still planted in her belly and her mouth was a bloody gash. Her eyes started into nothing. The snake slithered across the floor and rose up in front of the barbarian, hissing and spitting.

It would have struck but, at that very moment, Natali plucked the gemstone from the eye of the statue. The floor shook and dust rained from the ceiling. The living snake darted forward even as its body vanished in a puff of smoke. The fangs, dripping deadly venom, were mere inches from Redgar's chest when the head of the snake turned to ash and broke apart on a phantom breeze.

Redgar slumped against the base of the statue and breathed a sigh.

"We are forever in your debt, Hathor," Kreeger said. He put out a hand and Redgar clasped it.

Brom stood to one side looking mutinous. He blamed Redgar for the deaths of his comrades and, in a way, Redgar supposed he was right. Not that it mattered much to Redgar. To make matters worse, Kreeger had set the

Eye of the Serpent into a silver chain and hung it around the Hathor's neck. The green gemstone winked in the light as Redgar said his farewells to Kreeger. Natali stood at his side, bathed and properly dressed for the first time in days. The Brotherhood had outfitted them with clothes, many day's provisions, and a mule for their journey.

The big barbarian pumped Kreeger's hand and thanked him for the provisions. Kreeger only shook his head. "Just promise me you will see to the safe keeping of that stone, or its destruction. I was foolish to keep it in the city. It can no longer stay here. Sooner or later, the worshipers of Set will regroup and they will be on the hunt for the stone. You must make certain it is never found."

"I'll toss it in the deepest canyon I find upon my travels," Redgar assured him and, with a wave of his hand, escorted Natali from the stone house of the Brotherhood, through the winding lanes of Tehette, to the northern stair that climbed down from the soaring city to the wide, wind swept wastes of the Caladhasi Deserts.

ABOUT THE AUTHOR

Willard Black is the cantankerous author of numerous sword and sorcery adventures. He lives on six acres in southern Montana with a pair of mongrel dogs and his testy old biddy of a wife. He published the first Savage Realms stories in the late 80's during the height of the fantasy adventure craze. He's been playing video games since Pac-Man and when he's not writing, Willard can be found grinding in Conan Exiles. He does not do interviews.

AFTERWORD

We were a little late this month but we hope the result was worth the wait. If you enjoyed the latest issue, please let us know by leaving a review on Amazon. Reviews helps other like-minded readers discover Savage Realms Monthly and that puts coin in the coffers so we can pay future talent. And the best part is, it doesn't cost you a copper penny.

We want to sincerely thank you for picking up Savage Realms and we promise we'll be back next month with another exciting crop of axe wielding barbarians for your reading pleasure.

If you want to be notified of upcoming issues, simply click this link to be added to our mailing list. We'll let you know when the next issue hits the stands and we promise no spam. Ever.

Until next time, keep your swords sharp!

Are you a sword and sorcery fan? Do you pen tales of savages and wizards in your spare time? Have you always wanted to be a published author but have no idea where to start? Literary Rebel is seeking talented writers to feature in Savage Realms Monthly! The best part… We pay!

Send us your best sword and sorcery themed tale of no more than ten thousand (10,000) words and, if we like it, we'll pay for first publishing rights. Don't worry, you as the author will retain the copyright to all characters and locales so you are free to publish stories within your fictional universe in other publications in the future. We'll even link to any websites, social media, or storefronts you desire.

http://www.literaryrebel.com/savage-submissions/